Kaherí:io's Lacrosse Stick

Written and Illustrated by
David Kanietakeron Fadden

Translation by
Kaweienón:ni Cook

Native North American
Travelling College

This book provided
with the support of

ONTARIO**POWER**
GENERATION

1

Early one Saturday morning there was a knock on the front door of Kaherí:io's house. Kaherí:io opened the door and saw all of his friends with their lacrosse sticks. Tehonatákhe asked, "Can you come and play?"

Entákta, ohrhon'kè:ne Tehonatákhe iahahnhoháia'ke Kaherí:io tsi thonónhsote. Nó:nen Kaherí:io wahahnhotón:ko Tehonatákhe wahori'wanóntonhse, "Kaherí:io. Íhsere kenh taekiatshihkwà:eke?"

3

Kaherí:io's Ista said, "You can go. Don't go far and come back before supper time." Kaherí:io grabbed his lacrosse stick from the porch and ran with his friends to the field.

Kaherí:io ro'nisténha wa'è:ron, "Was. Enwá:ton, ne'k tsi tóhsa sótsi í:non iénhse tánon enséhsewe ohén:ton tsi niió:re o'karahsnéha enkekhwà:ren".

Kaherí:io's friend Rarihwenhá:wi was playing with a different kind of stick. The lacrosse stick was made from wood.

Kaherí:io ronatén:ro Rarihwenhá:wi ó:ia ne' ní:ioht ne raò:hien. Ó:iente ionnià:ton.

7

Kaherí:io asked Rarihwenhá:wi where he got that stick. Rarihwenhá:wi said; "My tota made it for me. It's made from wood. Cool, eh?"

Kaherí:io wahorì'wanòn:tonhse ne Rarihwenhá:wi, "Ka'nontáhshawe ne sá:hien?" Rariwenhá:wi wahèn:ron, "Raksótha wahrón:ni. Ó:iente ionnià:ton. Ióhskats wáhe?"

Kaherí:io got dropped off at his grandparent's house. His totas were sitting on the porch waiting for him. "Shé:kon."

10

Kaherí:io rohsotnéha iahonwaia'titáhko. Tetsiá:ron ahskwen'nà:ke thnítskote ronwahá:re. "Shé:kon", wahnì:ron.

"Tota, who is this?" Kaherí:io asked as he pointed to a picture on the wall. His grandfather said, "That's me. I played a lot of lacrosse when I was a young man."

12

"Tota, ónhka ne' kí:ken raià:tare?"
Rohsótha wahèn:ron, "Í:i kià:tare.
É:so se's tekatshihkwà:eks
ken'shitewakiòn:ah."

Kaherí:io's grandfather showed him his old lacrosse stick. Kaherí:io asked his grandfather if he knew where to buy a wooden lacrosse stick. His grandfather said; "Let's go for a walk. I'll show you how to get one."

14

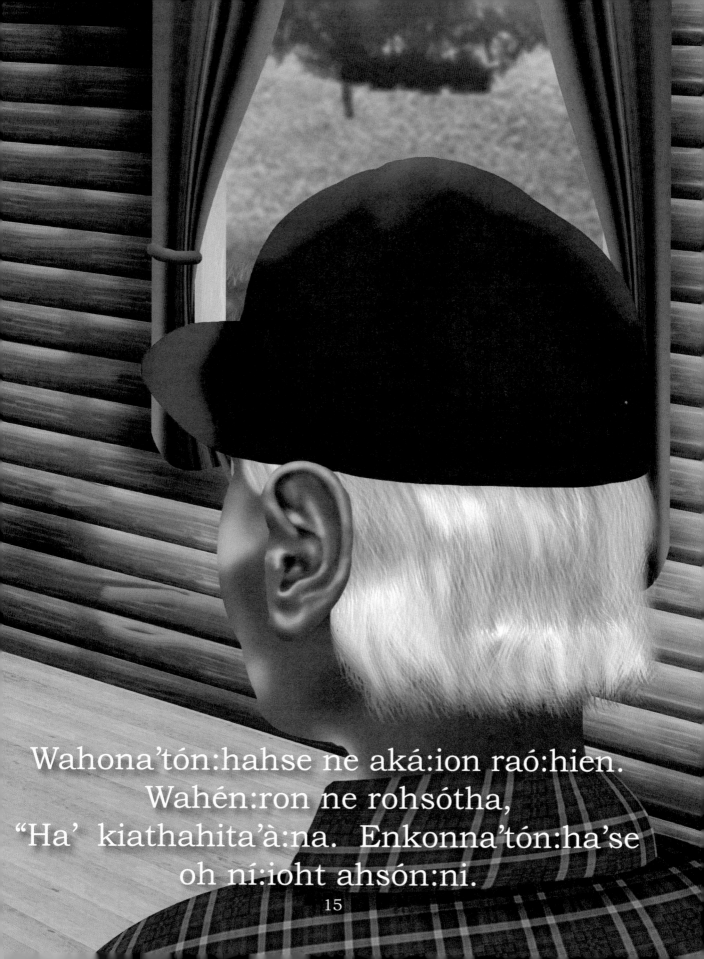

Wahona'tón:hahse ne aká:ion raó:hien.
Wahén:ron ne rohsótha,
"Ha' kiathahita'à:na. Enkonna'tón:ha'se
oh ní:ioht ahsón:ni.

They followed a trail into the woods when Tota put his hand on a big tree and said: "This is what our Lacrosse sticks are made from, the hickory tree."

Kahrhà:kon iahá:newe so'k kakwirowá:nen iahaié:na ne rohsótha. Wahèn:ron, "Onennóhkara ionnià:ton ne Tewa'á:raton teiontshihkwaékstha kà:ien.

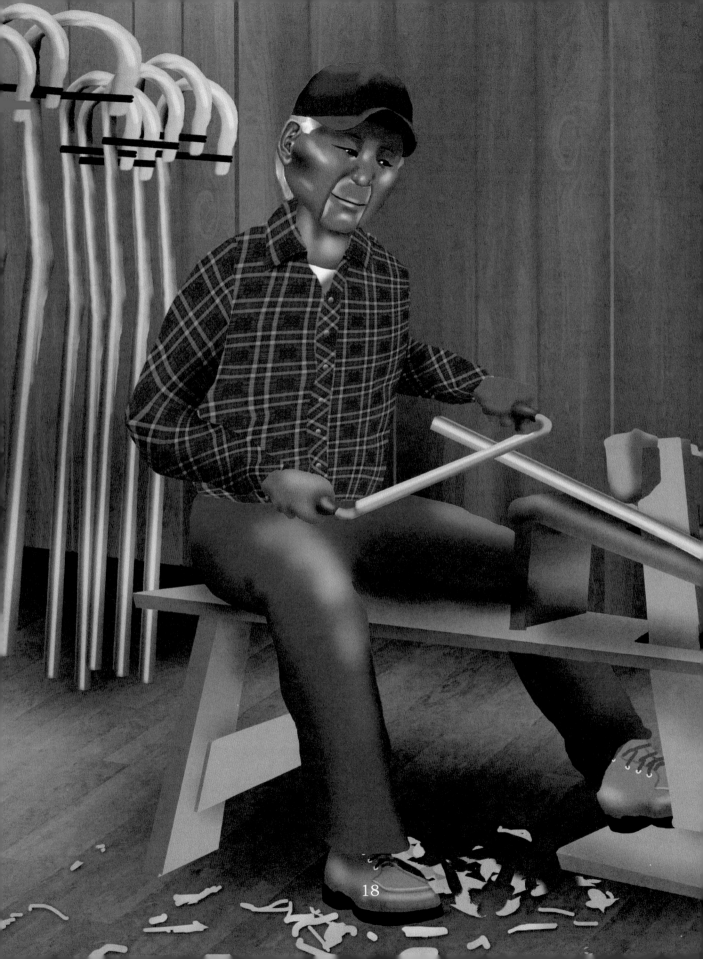

In the workshop Tota shows Kaherí:io how a stick is made. "First, you bend the wood," Tota said. "Then we sit on this horse bench and start carving the stick into a nice shape."

Wahèn:ron ne Tóta, "Kiokierénhton, tenhtshà:kete ne kà:hien. So'k wanitskwahrà:tsheres ensákien tánon enhskwè:taren tsi niió:re kaieron'tí:io".

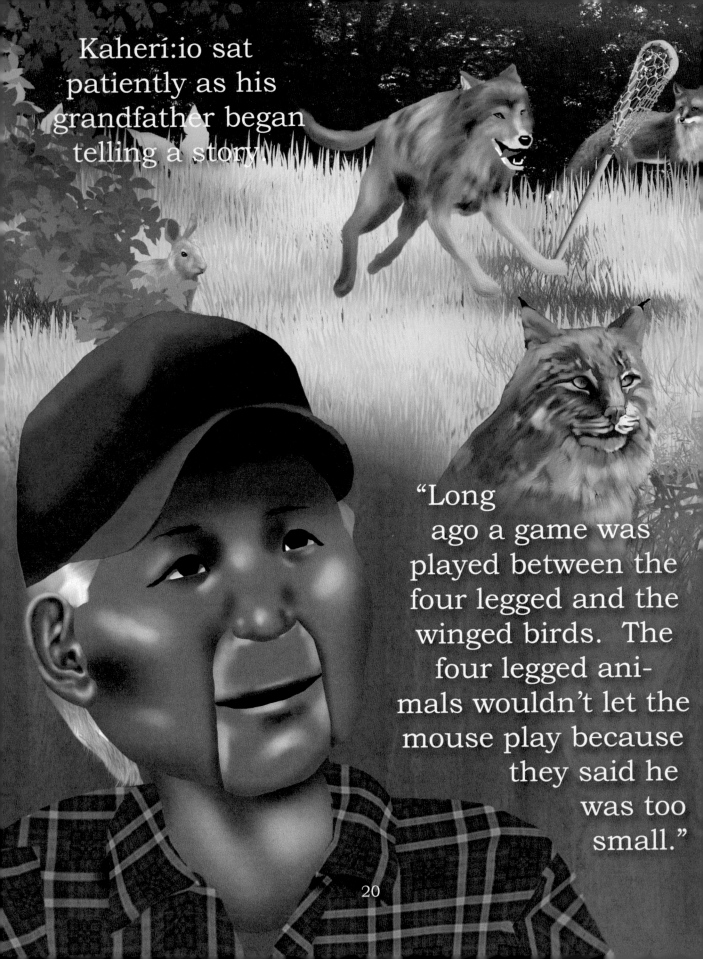

Kaherí:io sat patiently as his grandfather began telling a story.

"Long ago a game was played between the four legged and the winged birds. The four legged animals wouldn't let the mouse play because they said he was too small."

20

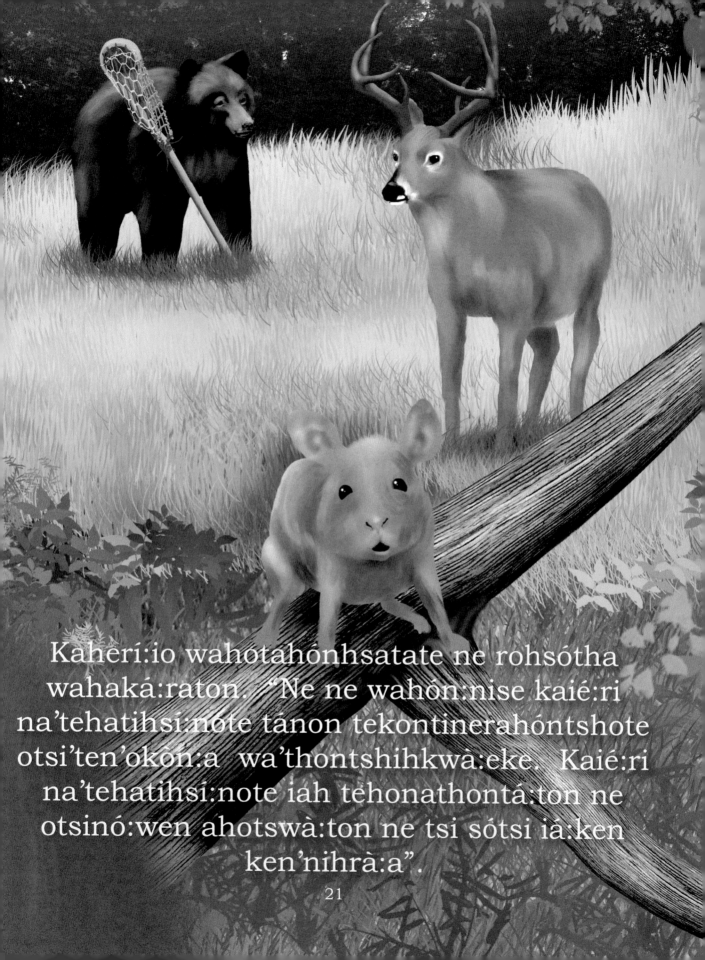

Kaherí:io wahótahónhsatate ne rohsótha
wahaká:raton. "Ne ne wahòn:nise kaié:ri
na'tehatihsí:note tánon tekontinerahóntshote
otsi'ten'okòn:a wa'thontshihkwà:eke. Kaié:ri
na'tehatihsí:note iah tehonathontá:ton ne
otsinó:wen ahotswà:ton ne tsi sótsi iá:ken
ken'nihrà:a".

"The birds let him play on their team. They gave him wings made from leather from the water drum." Grandpa continued: "The mouse became a bat and won the game for the birds because he was very fast. It didn't matter that he was small."

"Otsi'ten'okòn:a
wahonwaríhon raotinén:ra
nonkwá:ti ahátswa'te.
Kana'tsió:wi aoné:hon
wáhontste onerahónt-
sha wahonnón:ni tánon
wa'thon-
wanerahontshó:ten
ne otsinó:wen.
Tsikera'wístak wahá:ton
ne otsinó:wen tánon
wahontkwé:ni ne
otsi'ten'okòn:a né:e
tsi kwah í:ken tsi
raia'tahsnó:re. Aronhákien
tsi ken'nihrà:a."

23

Kaherí:io watched his grandmother lace the stick to make the net on the lacrosse stick. She said: "Lacrosse is sometimes played for our elders and healers. The game gives strength to our medicine."

Wahshakoterò:roke ne rohsótha wa'kion'á:raton ne kà:hien. Wa'è:ron ne rohsótha, "Sewakié:rens tewa'á:raton tenhontshihkwà:eke ne ionkhihsothokòn:a tánon tsi niká:ien ionkhiiatetsien'énhstha raotirihwà:ke. Enkonwati'satsténhseron ne onkwanonhkwa'òn:we."

24

Early next morning Kaherí:io woke to a surprise. His grandparents gave him the wooden lacrosse stick. Tota told him; "Always remember that the creator loves to watch lacrosse and you should always play with a good mind and play fair."

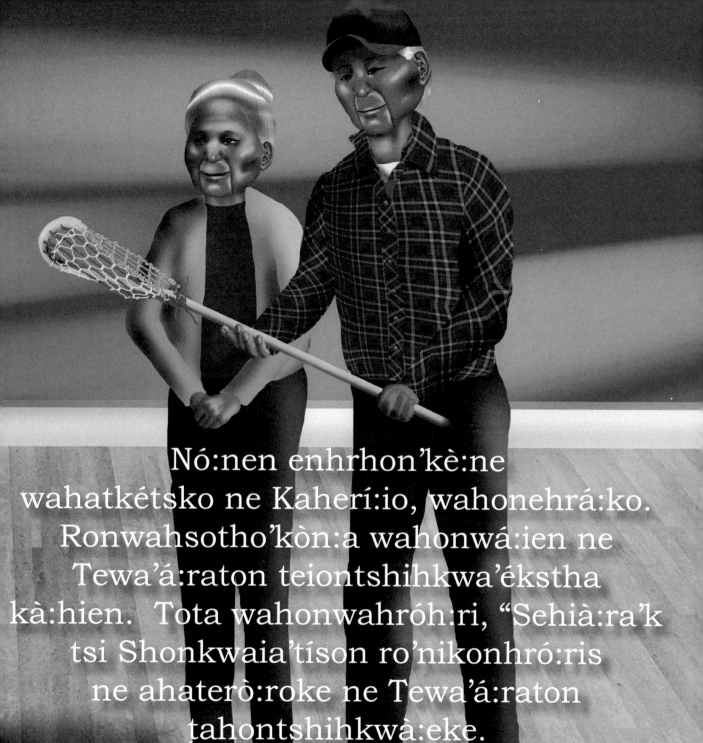

Nó:nen enhrhon'kè:ne
wahatkétsko ne Kaherí:io, wahonehrá:ko.
Ronwahsotho'kòn:a wahonwá:ien ne
Tewa'á:raton teiontshihkwa'ékstha
kà:hien. Tota wahonwahróh:ri, "Sehià:ra'k
tsi Shonkwaia'tíson ro'nikonhró:ris
ne ahaterò:roke ne Tewa'á:raton
tahontshihkwà:eke.
Kióhton ka'nikonhrí:io énsatste nó:nen
tenhsatshihkwà:eke tánon tóhsa
nenwén:ton enhse'nikónhrha'te.

Kaherí:io, his tota and Rákeni all went to
the field and played catch for a
long, long time.

So'k ki' rohsótha tánon ro'níha
akwé:kon kahentà:ke tánon karì:wes
ia'thonhthénno'ke.

28

The Native North American Travelling College has been at the forefront of cultural education and revitalization. It was established on the Akwesasne Mohawk Territory in 1974 under the name North American Indian Travelling College by Ernest Kaientaronkwen Benedict and Michael Kanentakeron Mitchell.

The Native North American Travelling College continues to evolve to meet the needs of a changing community. We need more than ever to promote and preserve our language culture and history, not only for our own sake, but to foster a greater appreciation and understanding in the outside community.

This picture book is the third of a series based on the life and experiences of a young Mohawk boy named Kaheri:io. The book concept was from Kaheri:io's real grandfather, Russell Karoniateh Roundpoint, former director of NNATC.

About the author and illustrator

DAVID KANIETAKERON FADDEN, Wolf Clan Mohawk, grew up in a family of artists, naturalists, and storytellers. His illustrations have appeared in books, periodicals, animations, and on television. He lives with his family on Kawenoke, also known as Cornwall Island, at Akwesasne.

About the Translator

KAWEIENÓN:NI (MARGARET) COOK belongs to the Snipe Clan of the Onondaga Nation. She works as a Kanein'keha specialist with the Akwesasne Mohawk Board of Education. She is Certified in Iroquois Linguistics through Syracuse University.

1 Ronathahon:ni Lane
Akwesasne, Ontario K6H 5R7

P.O. Box 273
Hogansburg, NY 13655

Made in the USA
Middletown, DE
06 July 2022